The Ice-Cream Cowboys

Adrian Boote

Illustrated by Tim Archbold

D1147443

Look out for the
Madcap Moonwood adventures!

The Lemonade Genie
The Ice Cream Cowboys
The Strawberry Sorcerer
The Lollipop Knight

To all at Leighfield Primary School A.B.

ORCHARD BOOKS
96 Leonard Street, London EC2A 4XD
Orchard Books Australia
14 Mars Road, Lane Cove, NSW 2066
First published in Great Britain in 2000
First paperback edition 2001
Text © Adrian Boote 2000
Illustrations © Tim Archbold 2000
The rights of Adrian Boote to be identified as the author
and Tim Archbold as the illustrator of this work
have been asserted by them in accordance with the
Copyright, Designs and Patents Act, 1988.
A CIP catalogue record for this book is available
from the British Library.
ISBN 1 84121 011 0 (hbk)
ISBN 1 84121 013 7 (pbk)
1 3 5 7 9 10 8 6 4 2 (hbk)
1 3 5 7 9 10 8 6 4 2 (pbk)
Printed in Great Britain

CONTENTS

1
THE MAX DAGGERS GANG

George Dobbs was a brilliant worrier. He worried about anything and everything. He worried that his pet hamster, Stringfellow, was really a fat vampire bat whose wings had dropped off. He worried that evil tooth fairies wanted to steal all his teeth before they had even fallen out. He worried that monsters hid under his bed at night. Ugly slobbering monsters, that sucked people's brains out of their ears through a straw. Most of all, George worried that Terrible Things were about to happen to him. But of course, they never did… Until one hot Sunday in the summer holidays.

It had been a quiet day. Worryingly,
George had only found three things to
worry about. He worried that his hair was
growing unusually quickly, and he was
turning into a werewolf.
Then Stringfellow bit him,
and he worried that he was
turning into a were-hamster.
Then he found a spot on his
nose. A huge pink
spot that looked as
if it might grow
into a huge pink
rhinoceros horn. George
worried that he had caught
Pink Rhinoceros Disease –
and no one would ever look
at him again without
screaming.
Then he discovered
it wasn't a spot at all, but
a gloop of strawberry jam.

"I'm bored," Mum whinged. "There's nothing to do. Nothing *ever* happens in Moonwood. If Moonwood had its own newspaper, it would only be half a page long. And even that would be empty. Except once a year, when Moonwood won the Most Boring Town in England award."

"Moonwood isn't boring," George said, darkly. "Terrible Things happen here. Remember the time that double-decker bus dropped out of the sky and straight through the roof of Halfbottle and Son's ice cream factory? Dad was Assistant Chief

Vanilla Inspector. He was almost drowned in dairy cream sludge. It took hours to thaw him out. And he's hardly spoken a word since."

"He's hardly spoken a word *ever*," Mum muttered.

Dad looked as if he were about to say something…but the very idea seemed to scare him. So he just sat there and read his favourite magazine, *Gloom Monthly*.

"It rained double-decker buses on Drizzle's Hairdressers, too," George went on, worriedly. "*And* Trudge's Toffee Emporium. No one knows why. But if *that* can happen in Moonwood, *any* Terrible Thing can happen."

Mum shrugged, pulled a sulky face and looked outside.

Glumchurch Road was silent. Except for Mr Trudge next door, who lounged in his garden sucking a toffee. And Mrs Drizzle who sat in an upstairs window across the road,

blow-drying her hair. She was always

blow-drying her hair. It was her hobby.

"I'm bored," Mum moaned. "There's nothing to do. Nothing ever happens in Moonwood…"

But then, something *did* happen.

George heard someone laughing. A chilling howl of a laugh. A laugh George knew…

He looked outside. And in that moment, the biggest worry of his life exploded all over him.

"It's Max Daggers and his gang!" he gasped.

Max Daggers, Sam Snodgrass, Little Pete Sweet and the McCoy boys, Roy and Roger, were George's classmates – and the biggest troublemakers in the whole of Moonwood County Primary School. The terrors of the playground. The frightful five. But what were they doing here, in Glumchurch Road?

They seemed to be happily swinging on the gates of Underweather Farm. But George wasn't fooled. They were here to make trouble. It was all they *ever* did.

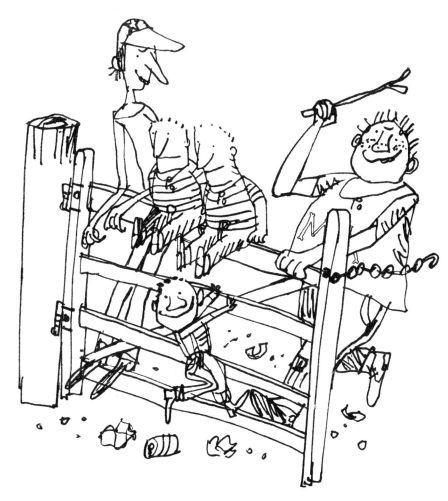

Max Daggers was a master of wickedness. His black imagination bubbled with despicable trouble-making ideas.

It wasn't just George Dobbs, it was *everyone* who worried about Max Daggers.

Sam Snodgrass was the gang's insect keeper. He once took a boxful of chocolates and filled them all with insects. He made spider swirls, beetle truffles, crunchy bluebottle clusters. George's teacher, Mr Cheese, ate almost the whole box before he realised.

Little Pete Sweet was the slimy creatures expert.

He trained worms, frogs and snails to sneak into other people's pockets and bags, and up legs and down necks. Especially Mr Cheese's.

The McCoy boys were water pistol sharpshooters – the deadliest around. They could soak you to the bone in the blinking of an eye. Mr Cheese had been soaked so often, he was hardly ever dry.

But what wickedness did the Max Daggers Gang have planned for the people of Glumchurch Road? George didn't dare think about it.

The tinkling music of an ice cream van sounded outside. It was an odd, spooky tune – and George wasn't sure why, but he felt another worry coming on.

"You know what? I fancy an ice cream," Mum said.

George gulped in shock. Mum hadn't eaten ice cream since that terrible day when Dad was dairy cream sludged.

"Mmm…" agreed Dad.

 George double-gulped in horror. Dad had actually spoken. Almost.

"Just pop out and get three ice creams, George. There's a good lad," Mum said.

Now George was terror-struck. He couldn't possibly *just pop out.* What if Max Daggers saw him? Didn't Mum know the Terrible Things he could do?

Max Daggers had once slipped a mouse into a bread roll where a hot dog should have been. What if he kidnapped Stringfellow, and turned him into a hamster salad sandwich?

"Are you listening to me, George Dobbs?" Mum whined. "Nobody *ever* listens to me."

George was so full up with worry, he couldn't speak. His brain babbled. His tongue tangled up. And, as Mum hurried him through the front door, all he could do was...gulp.

Suddenly, George was outside in Glumchurch Road.

He knew the Max Daggers Gang were close. He couldn't see them, but he could feel their eyes, staring at him.

George's worry was coming true...

2
HANDSOME JOHN
AND ONE-EYED WAYNE

It was a perfect summer's afternoon. The sky was perfectly blue. The air was perfectly still. Everything was... *too* perfect.

George had a worrying feeling a dirty great thunderstorm was about to blow up.

There was a pair of wellies in the porch. He pulled them on, and grabbed an umbrella.

Then he had another clever thought. If he hid underneath the umbrella, the Max Daggers Gang wouldn't recognise him.

He put the umbrella up.

Now, if only he could get to the ice cream van and back without drawing attention to himself...

He took a deep breath, and ran. But then…

"Well, if it ain't George Dobbs!" a voice cried.

George turned.

But Max Daggers wasn't there. Nobody was there.

"Don't you worry, George," the voice laughed. "Ain't nobody here but you…"

"…and us," grumbled another voice.

Then George realised. The voices were coming from inside the ice cream van.

It was a battered old van, the colour of vanilla ice cream, and decorated with pictures of happy smiling cows. A sign on the front read:

The ICE CREAM COWBOYS

And inside it were the two ugliest ice cream men George had ever seen.

They both wore cowboy hats, black and white checked shirts, and sheriffs' badges with their names on: JOHN and WAYNE.

John was as big
as a grizzly bear.
He had enormous
eyeballs, too
big for his head.
His nose was flat,
as if someone
had punched it
inside out. His
mouth was
a ferocious frown.

Wayne was so skinny
he was hardly there. He
had a zigzagging smile
full of ugly green
teeth, like broken
old gravestones.
A weedy orange
beard sprouted
from his chin.
"We're John and
Wayne Mountainside,"
smiled Wayne.

"I'm Handsome John," growled John. "And he's One-eyed Wayne."

George looked closely at Wayne.

"He's got *two* eyes," he said.

"Oh? You telling me I can't count?" snapped John.

George stared up at Handsome John's mad face and gulped.

"N-No," he stuttered. "I wouldn't dare."

And he didn't dare tell John he wasn't handsome, either.

"Don't you worry about Handsome John," chortled Wayne. "He don't bite. Much."

"I'm not worried," said George. "I never worry."

"Sure you do!" sniggered Wayne. "I'd say you're mighty worried about the Max Daggers Gang!"

At the very mention of Max Daggers' name, George turned as white as a ghost in a snowstorm. Wayne laughed, a scratchy, wheezy little laugh. John just grunted.

"OK. You're right," George sulked. "I'm *always* worrying. I collect worries like other boys collect football stickers. I wish I didn't."

"Maybe Handsome John and me can help," smiled Wayne.

"What can you do?" George asked. "You're only ice cream men."

"We're the Ice Cream Cowboys!" John roared. "The most magnificent trouble-shooting good guys in the whole ice cream world!"

"You got problems? Our ice creams can fix 'em," smiled Wayne. "We got every flavour from Boiled Buffalo and Beans to Pickled Porcupine Pie and Fresh Squeezed Skunk. And they don't just taste good. They do magical things you wouldn't believe. Poke your tongue into our ice cream and you'll get a mouthful of miracles..."

George wasn't impressed. They sounded more like dollops of disgustingness.

"Miracles won't stop *me* worrying," he said. "I'm a worrying genius. All of us Dobbses are. Dad's such a scaredy cat he daren't even speak. And Mum, well, she's the biggest misery pants in Moonwood. I've never *once* heard her laugh. I reckon she's forgotten how."

"Leave it to the Ice Cream Cowboys," Wayne grinned. "You want to hear your ma laugh? Give her this…"

He held out a cone filled with gruesome green ice cream. George took it.

"Mint flavoured ice cream?" he asked.

"Nope," chuckled Wayne, "Cactus Crunch."

George stared at it. Sure enough, thousands of tiny cactus spikes were poking out.

"It's full of prickles," he said.

"They're not prickles," said Wayne. "They're *tickles.* Cactus Crunch is the tickliest ice cream of 'em all. One lick, and your ma'll laugh till her lips catch fire."

George looked doubtful.

"And this'll get your pa talking…"

Wayne handed George a cone filled with disgusting brown ice cream.

"Chocolate?" asked George.

"Rattlesnake Ripple," smiled Wayne.

Rattlesnake Ripple

George listened. The ice cream was alive with tiny hissings and rattlings. "Is it…poisonous?" asked George. Wayne tee-heed. "It *sounds* poisonous. But that's just *NOISINESS.* Rattlesnake Ripple is the noisiest ice cream ever. One taste, and your pa'll talk-talk-talk till his teeth turn blue."

George looked worried.

"George Dobbs, you got so many worries inside you, they're holding you down like a bellyful of rocks." Wayne laughed. "You need this…"

He held out a cone of ghastly pink ice cream.

"That's *definitely* raspberry," George said.

"Sure is," chuckled Wayne. "It's Raspberry Ice *Dynamite*. It'll blast all your worries away with one almighty KABOOM! And when the smoke clears, you'll feel good all over. And you'll do things, and wonder why you never dared do them before. Nothing'll stop you. Not even the Max Daggers Gang…"

Very carefully, George took the Raspberry Ice Dynamite.

It looked just like raspberry ice cream. If there was an almighty KABOOM! in there, George couldn't see it. And he wasn't sure he dared eat a bellyful of exploding ice cream.

"I don't mean to be ungrateful," he said, "but can't I just have three ordinary, unmagical ice creams instead?"

But the Ice Cream Cowboys had already gone.

George was alone in Glumchurch Road, holding an umbrella in one hand and three ice creams in the other.

"Look, Gang!" said a familiar voice. "It's George Dobbs! Let's give him something to worry about!"

It's George Dobbs

Before George could move, someone
had snatched his umbrella, and shut
George's head inside it. He felt many
hands spinning him around, until he was
so dizzy he fell over.

"Be very afraid, Dobbs," the voice said.
"Looks like it's a man-eating umbrella
you've got there…"

The voice laughed a chilling howl of
a laugh.

"Max Daggers," whimpered George.

3
CACTUS CRUNCH AND RATTLESNAKE RIPPLE

George fought off his umbrella just in time to see the Max Daggers Gang disappearing over a wall into Underweather Farm. He spotted something pink in Max Daggers' hand...and soon discovered what it was. George only had two ice creams left. Max Daggers had stolen his Raspberry Ice Dynamite.

George sighed. It wasn't the worst thing they could have done. Sam Snodgrass could have filled his underpants with spiders. Little Pete Sweet could have put slugs in his ears. The McCoy boys could have given him the soaking of his life.

But...why hadn't they?

George knew why. This was only the beginning. *They would be back...*

George gulped. And gulped again. He gulped loud enough for the whole street to hear. Then he realised he was being watched.

A frizzy-haired Mrs Drizzle was frowning at him from an upstairs window. Mr Trudge, meanwhile, glared at him and crunched his toffee, crossly. George realised how stupid he must look, sitting in the road on a scorching day, holding two ice creams and an umbrella, gulping.

On any other day, it would have worried him that his neighbours thought he was a complete twit. But today, he had bigger worries than that. What Terrible Things were the Max Daggers Gang going to do to him...and when?

He ran home, handed Mum and Dad the two remaining ice creams, then hurried to his room to do some worrying.

Minutes later, strange noises drifted upstairs. They sounded like...voices. But George didn't recognise them. One was deep and rumbly. The other, shrieky...like laughter.

George had the strangest thought. Those Ice Cream Cowboys couldn't have been telling the truth, could they? Those weird ice creams couldn't really be magical – could they?

George had to know.

He ran downstairs…and found Mum and Dad, smiling enormous cheeky smiles, their mouths smothered in ice cream, as thick as a clown's lipstick.

"George!" exclaimed Dad. "That was the most *marvellous* ice cream ever! I don't know what it did to my mouth, but I feel like I've got a *brand new tongue* in there – and I just can't shut it up! And as for Mum… well! She's gone completely and utterly—"

He was interrupted by an almighty eardrum-shattering laugh, like the screeching of a million mad chimpanzees. Incredibly, it was coming out of Mum.

George stared. His gob was smacked, his flabber ghasted and his bam completely boozled. He didn't know whether to laugh…or worry.

He worried.

"Oh, do cheer up, George!" Dad exclaimed. "Or I'll give you a jolly good tickling!"

He grinned a wicked grin, and waggled his fingers menacingly.

Now, George didn't know how to cheer up. It wasn't something he did very often. He tried pulling a cheerful face, but it was useless. He looked like someone who'd accidentally sat down on a custard pie.

Mum laughed. She howled like a hysterical hyena and fat tears of laughter squirted everywhere.

"As for you, Mrs Dobbs..." Dad went on, with a twinkle in his eye, "I've been wondering. When was the last time you and I enjoyed a really good piggyback?"

"*Mr Dobbs!*" Mum tittered. "Do you think we dare?"

"Mrs Dobbs, I feel so marvellous, I could piggyback from here to Moonwood High Street!"

And he hoisted Mum on to his back and galloped off, around the sofa, into the hall, out of the front door, and away down Glumchurch Road. And as he galloped, he sang, loudly. And Mum laughed so hard she almost burst.

Mrs Drizzle watched in amazement, and her frizzy hair collapsed around her shoulders like strings of soggy spaghetti.

Mr Trudge simply spluttered and choked on his toffee in disbelief.

As for George, he didn't know what else to do but gawp, open-mouthed. A bee flew into his mouth, buzzed around it, then flew off again. George didn't notice.

He hadn't believed the Ice Cream Cowboys. But they had told the truth. The Cactus Crunch and the Rattlesnake Ripple were magical, all right. And

that meant the Raspberry Ice Dynamite must be magical, too. And what had One-eyed Wayne said about the Raspberry Ice Dynamite?

It'll blast your worries away with one almighty KABOOM! And when the smoke clears, you'll feel good all over. And you'll do things, and wonder why you never dared do them before...

But Max Daggers had stolen the Raspberry Ice Dynamite – and there wasn't much Max Daggers hadn't dared do before.

What would he do *now?*

4
RASPBERRY ICE
DYNAMITE

That night, George lay in bed, unable to sleep. It didn't help that Mum and Dad were being noisy downstairs.

"Mrs Dobbs, there's something I've been wanting to tell you for *ages*," he heard Dad say. "You're the most *beautiful* woman I've *ever seen*. Your eyes are as blue as an island paradise sky. Your lips are as tender as rosebuds on a dewy spring morn. Your ears are as big as pie dishes, but I like them like that."

"Oooh, Mr Dobbs, I'm the happiest woman alive," Mum giggled.

George sighed. He almost wished Mum and Dad were their miserable old selves again.

But what really kept him awake that night was the worry that the Max Daggers Gang were about to do something truly terrible. At the slightest sound, he shot bolt upright, as if he had springs in his pyjamas. He didn't dare fall asleep.

But in the end, he did. And in his dreams, the Max Daggers Gang tried to blow him up with Raspberry Ice Dynamite…

Next morning arrived with a loud cock-a-doodle-doo! In fact, whatever was cock-a-doodle-dooing was doing it so loudly, it could almost have been in George's bedroom.

Slowly, George realised it *was* in his bedroom. He peeped one eye out from under the bedclothes… and there, on his bedside table, was an enormous cockerel.

George sprang up, and fumbled for his slippers. Something cracked and squidged under his left foot. His slipper was full of eggs. His other slipper felt too tight, and wouldn't keep still. That was because it wasn't a slipper at all. George was trying to squeeze his right foot into a squawking chicken. Suddenly, George's room was *full* of squawking chickens.

Before he had a chance to say, "The Max Daggers Gang!" there was a terrified shriek outside.

George ran to the window…and gasped.

Glumchurch Road had been taken over by the animals of Underweather Farm. Herds of bemused sheep filled the road like a huge woolly traffic jam. Families of ducks waddled along the pavements. In every garden, horses munched their way through lawns and flowerbeds. And in the middle of it all, fat purple-faced Farmer Underweather hopped about, panic-stricken.

Mrs Drizzle was outside too. She wore a nightie and fluffy slippers. Her hair was piled up and trapped under a huge hair-net, like a string bag full of candy floss. And she was shrieking.

"Pigs!" she cried. "I've been invaded by pigs!"

George dressed quickly and ran outside.

"I woke up, and there was a pig, *in my bed!*" Mrs Drizzle wailed. "There was one in my wardrobe too, *wearing my clothes!* And there was an *enormous* one in my bath, wallowing in something thick and sticky and stinky…"

She suddenly froze.

Mr Trudge was staggering out of his front door.

He looked like he had escaped from the jaws of a terrible beast. Great holes had been chomped in his pyjamas. His slippers were in tatters. But worse than that, he was now completely bald. His head was as smooth and shiny as an ice rink.

"*Mr Trudge!*" Mrs Drizzle exclaimed in horror. "Somebody's stolen your hair!"

At that moment, a goat trotted out of Mr Trudge's house, chomping Mr Trudge's wig as if it were a tuft of grass.

"That's not all," Mr Trudge mumbled, gummily. "It ate my false teeth, too."

The goat smiled at everyone with Mr Trudge's big toffee-chewing choppers.

George didn't know where to look. Everywhere he turned, there was chaos.

His mind raced.

The Max Daggers Gang had done all this. He knew it.

There they stood, outside Underweather Farm, laughing at all the trouble they had made. Thanks to George's Raspberry Ice Dynamite, it had been their most daring troublemaking morning ever.

And something told George they hadn't finished yet...

5
THE
DAISY SPECIAL

Everyone was too busy chasing farm
animals to notice the tinkling music of
the ice cream van. Everyone except
George. He recognised that spooky tune.

"John! Wayne! Thank goodness you're
here!" he gasped, as he ran to the
battered van. "It's Max Daggers. He ate
my Raspberry Ice Dynamite, and now
he's doing daring things he never dared
do before. You've got to stop him."

"Is that so?" snarled Handsome John.
"What can we do? We're just ice cream
men."

"No, you're not. You're the Ice Cream
Cowboys. The most magnificent trouble-
shooting good guys in the whole ice
cream world. And you've got to stop Max

Daggers before he gets even bigger troublemaking ideas…"

"Slow down, George," interrupted One-eyed Wayne. "Why should *we* stop him? Why don't *you*?"

"Me?" George asked. "Well, I… suppose I really *ought* to do something, but I…daren't."

"You're worried that Terrible Things might happen to you," John sneered.

"No, I'm not," said George.

"Answer me this, George Dobbs," said Wayne. "What kind of world would this be if *everyone* was like you? What if *no one* dared do the things they knew they ought to do?"

George sighed.

"You're right," he said. "I'm *very* worried that Terrible Things might happen to me."

"Yesterday, your ma and pa did things they never dared do before. Did Terrible Things happen to them?" asked Wayne. "No. They did not."

Wayne was right. Mum and Dad had had the time of their lives.

"But...what can I do?" asked George. "I can't stop the Max Daggers Gang single-handedly. I'd need a miracle. I'd need a whole *mouthful* of miracles..."

Handsome John and One-eyed Wayne looked at each other.

They thought for a moment. Then, slowly, Handsome John nodded.

He disappeared through two large swinging doors, into a strange fog-filled room at the back of the van.

Suddenly, George heard cows mooing. And the funny thing was, the mooing was coming from the strange room behind the swinging doors. It got louder and louder, and the van began to shake.

"Our ice creams have all kinds of miracles in 'em," Wayne began. "There's Apple and Alligator flavour. Eat that and your teeth turn big and spiky and spitting with wickedness. That'll scare the Max Daggers Gang. Or there's Banjo De luxe. Lick that and your mouth plays cowboy music every time you open it. That'll *really* scare 'em. Then there's Swamp Surprise. The surprise is, *it* eats *you.* Max Daggers sticks in his tongue, and it sucks him right in till he's gone for ever…"

George shuddered at the very idea.

"But the most miraculous ice cream of 'em all," Wayne whispered, "is the Daisy Special."

And at that moment, Handsome John burst through the swinging doors, a trail of mist behind him.

He held aloft an ice cream so perfect, so brilliantly white, that it dazzled and shone.

"What's a Daisy Special?" George asked.

"Daisy," said Wayne, "is our most special cow. When you milk her, it ain't milk that comes out. It's ice cream. And not just any old ice cream, neither. The best, the finest, most melt-in-the-mouth magicest ice cream that ever was."

George took the Daisy Special. Then he thought for a moment. He thought about the mooing noises he had heard.

"Are you saying that this ice cream has been squeezed straight out of a cow?" he asked.

"Sure," snarled John. "So what?"

"You've actually got a cow, right there, in your van?"

"Not *a* cow," laughed Wayne. "We got a whole herd of 'em."

George couldn't believe it. But then, he hadn't believed ice creams could be magical, either.

He stared at the Daisy Special. And very delicately, he touched it with his tongue…

It tasted delicious. But nothing magical happened.

"What sort of magic does it do?" he asked.

But the Ice Cream Cowboys had already gone.

And when George turned, the Max Daggers Gang stood in his way.

6
THε HAMSTεR-POWεRεD ROCKεT

The Max Daggers Gang were not a pretty sight.

Max Daggers was big and powerful, with a sneer that looked like his mouth was creeping up the side of his face.

Sam Snodgrass was as long and thin as a stick insect. He giggled stupidly, even when there was nothing to giggle about.

Little Pete Sweet looked like an ugly baby. He chomped bubble gum noisily, and blew big bubbles that popped all over his face.

The McCoy boys were short and wide and did nothing but stare, harder than rocks.

The whole gang held water pistols. MASSIVE water pistols, as big as cannons.

"We meet again, Dobbs," said Max Daggers. "I'm glad. I wanted to thank you for that weird ice cream I stole from you yesterday."

Sam Snodgrass giggled stupidly.

"I don't know what it did to me, but one minute I had belly-ache, the next I was burping raspberry smoke," Max

Daggers went on. "Then I turned into an evil genius, and sneaked farm animals into people's houses. It was the most brilliant thing I've ever done, Dobbs. And I reckon I couldn't have done it without your ice cream. So just to say thank you, we're going to blast you with my latest wicked invention…"

Slowly, the Max Daggers Gang aimed their water pistols.

George went cold all over.

"These are my Nasty Blasters," Max Daggers said. "They're like water pistols, but nastier. The McCoy boys have got frogspawn in theirs. Little Pete's fires real snails. Sam's got a whole ants' nest in his. And I've got your little furry hamster friend in mine…"

"No! Not Stringfellow!" gasped George.

Max Daggers smirked, enjoying the look of horror on George's face.

"Too late, Dobbs," he laughed. "Prepare to be blasted."

George was numb with panic. So numb, he couldn't even gulp. This was like all his worst worries rolled into one. Nothing else in his life would ever be as terrible as this.

Suddenly, he remembered.

He still had the Daisy Special. He licked it, and hoped for something magical to happen…

It didn't.

The Ice Cream Cowboys had lied. There was no magic in the Daisy Special.

George realised then that if he was going to stop the Max Daggers Gang, he'd have to do it *alone.* And at that moment, something miraculous *did* happen.

George smiled.

"Go on," he said.

"Blast me. I dare you…"

The McCoy boys were the first to squeeze their triggers.

But nothing happened.

Confused, they stared down the nozzles of their Nasty Blasters to see what had gone wrong… and then the Nasty Blasters fired. All over the McCoy boys.

They staggered about, screaming, their faces full of wriggly tadpole slime. Roy McCoy grabbed Little Pete Sweet, just as he was blowing his biggest ever

gummy bubble. Roger McCoy grabbed
Sam Snodgrass, who accidentally fired
his Nasty Blaster. The ants' nest flew out,
and millions of ants plastered themselves
on to Little Pete Sweet's bubble-gummy
face.

He squealed in panic, and accidentally
fired *his* Nasty Blaster. Six snails shot out
and stuck with horrible sucky
squelches on to Sam
Snodgrass's face.

He fell over,
shrieking.

"You've had it now, Dobbs," Max Daggers hissed. "Let's see how you like a faceful of hamster…"

He stared hard at George. His eyes narrowed.

But then something moved. Trapped inside the Nasty Blaster, a sad little Stringfellow caught George's eye.

"NOOO!!!"

George lunged forward, and thrust the Daisy Special – as if it were a great sword – straight down the barrel of the Nasty Blaster. And as Max Daggers fired, there was an explosion.

Stringfellow plopped on to the floor, dripping in ice cream. But Max Daggers shot high into the air, and flew away, across the rooftops. He hadn't blasted Stringfellow from the Nasty Blaster at all. Stringfellow had blasted *him.*

On and on Max Daggers flew, like the world's first hamster-powered rocket, from one end of the street to the other, until WALLOP! He crashed into the spire of St Edmund's Church. And there he clung, whimpering helplessly.

"MAX DAGGERS! GET DOWN OFF THAT CHURCH!" It was Superintendent Brickhouse from Moonwood Police Station.

"I'M ARRESTING YOU FOR THE KIDNAPPING OF ALL THE ANIMALS ON UNDERWEATHER FARM!"

He bellowed through his loudspeaker.

The rest of the Max Daggers Gang turned and fled.

The Daisy Special lay splattered across the road. George stared at it, and wondered...

"Isn't Moonwood *marvellous*?" Dad sighed. "You never know what's going to fall out of the sky next. One day it's double-decker buses. The next it's Max Daggers..."

Mum sniggered.

"What shall *we* do next, Mr Dobbs?" she asked excitedly.

Farmer Underweather ran by, chasing a duck.

"I feel like saying boo to a goose..." Dad grinned.

Mum let out a snorty chuckle. And off they went.

George laughed. A strange new

feeling came over him. Slowly he realised what it was. This was how you felt when you had nothing to worry about. And to think that, only yesterday, he had worried about  brain-sucking monsters, evil tooth fairies and vampire hamsters.

"Never again," George said to himself. "I, George Dobbs, faced the Max Daggers Gang, the biggest troublemakers in Moonwood…and nothing terrible happened to me. After that, what else in the world could I *possibly* worry about?"

Down at his feet, Stringfellow lapped up the last licks of the fast-melting Daisy Special. When he had finished, Stringfellow smiled up at George. It was a strange, fangy-toothed smile. The smile of a vampire…

"On the other hand…" George murmured.

That evening, nobody heard the strange music of the battered old ice cream van. But the Ice Cream Cowboys didn't mind.

"Another satisfied customer," One-eyed Wayne chuckled.

Handsome John just grunted.

And together they disappeared through the swinging doors, into the strange fog-filled room where the ice cream cows roamed.